The Silver Squawk Box

BY
CHARLOTTE GRAEBER

ILLUSTRATED BY
JOE BODDY

publishers since 1798

Thomas Nelson Publishers
Nashville • Camden • New York

It was almost dark. I hid in the bushes outside the shopping mall. I watched the entrance doors.

Suddenly I heard yelling. "Stop! Thief!"

I crouched down. My knees shook as I peered through the bushes.

The yelling got louder. "Catch that girl! Stop her!"

And louder. "Stop! Thief!"

Published in Nashville, Tennessee, by Thomas Nelson, Inc. and distributed in Canada by Lawson Falle, Ltd., Cambridge, Ontario.

Printed in the United States of America.

ISBN: 0-8407-6638-6

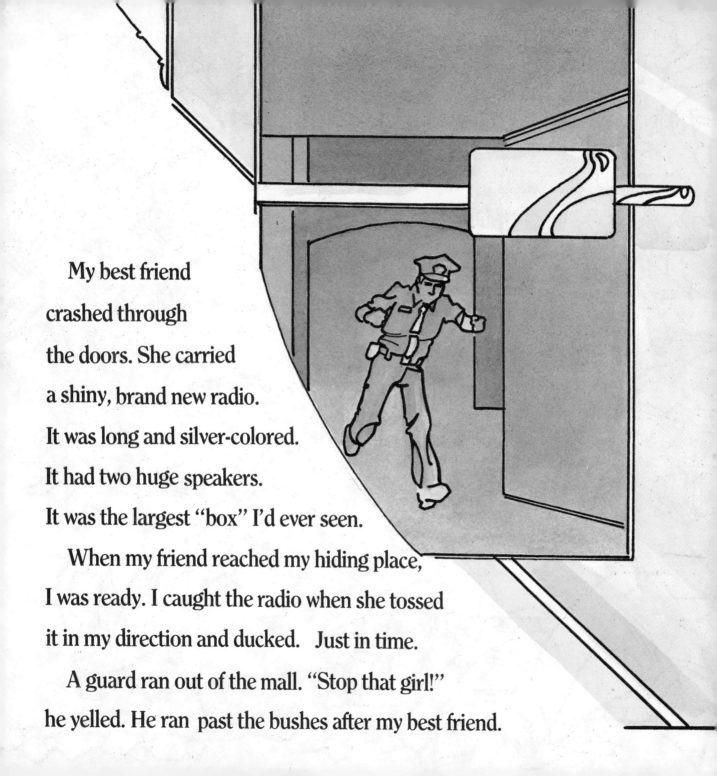

My best friend
crashed through
the doors. She carried
a shiny, brand new radio.
It was long and silver-colored.
It had two huge speakers.
It was the largest "box" I'd ever seen.

When my friend reached my hiding place,
I was ready. I caught the radio when she tossed
it in my direction and ducked.   Just in time.

A guard ran out of the mall. "Stop that girl!"
he yelled. He ran past the bushes after my best friend.

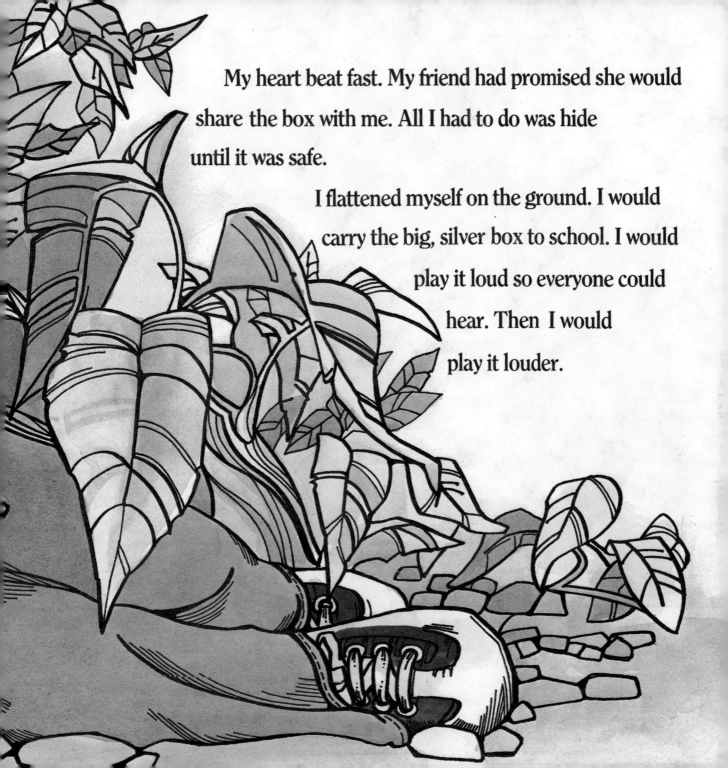

My heart beat fast. My friend had promised she would share the box with me. All I had to do was hide until it was safe.

I flattened myself on the ground. I would carry the big, silver box to school. I would play it loud so everyone could hear. Then I would play it louder.

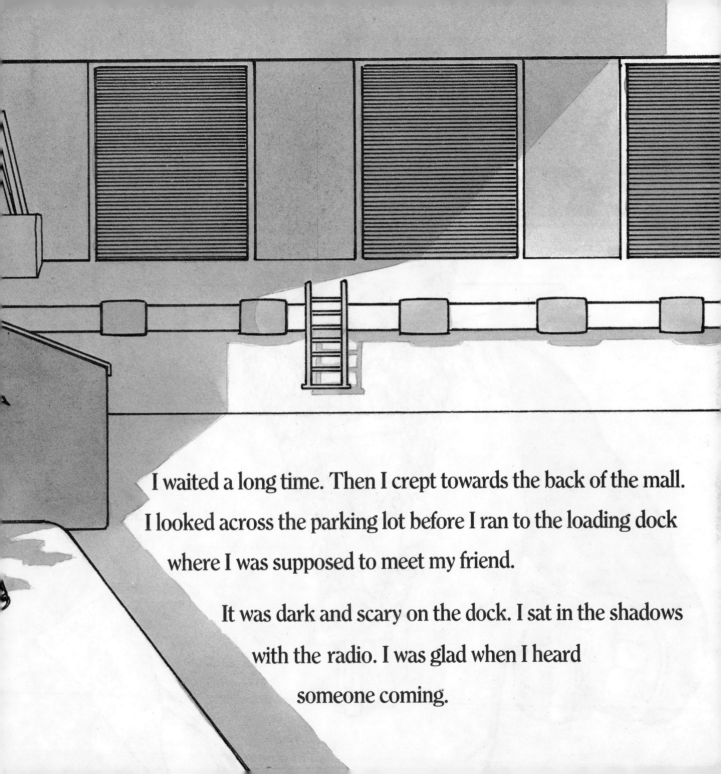

I waited a long time. Then I crept towards the back of the mall.
I looked across the parking lot before I ran to the loading dock
where I was supposed to meet my friend.

It was dark and scary on the dock. I sat in the shadows
with the radio. I was glad when I heard
someone coming.

"Over here!" I whispered. But it wasn't my best friend. It was someone much, much bigger. It was someone much, much wider. It was someone with a great, large shadow. It was Mr. T and he *saw* me!

"What are you doing here?" I croaked. I tried to hide the radio behind me.

"I'm pickin' up my new TV," he said. "What are you doin'?"

"I . . . I'm just leaving," I said. I grabbed the radio and jumped off the dock.

Mr. T stopped me with one arm. "That radio's got a price tag on it. Look's brand new to me."

Even if I am a girl, I don't like to cry.

When I feel tears coming,

I swallow hard.

"I didn't steal the radio—exactly," I said. Then I explained about hiding in the bushes. "See? I didn't take it from the store."

Mr. T shook his head. Then he reached for the radio. I swallowed hard. But there came the tears. Right on Mr. T's arm!

Mr. T ignored them. Instead he lifted my chin with his thumb. "You're no big wheel when you steal, little lady," he said. "You're just a flat tire."

I felt like a flat tire. Then I felt worse—like a tire with mud all over it.

Mr. T handed me the radio. "Ever heard of the commandment: 'You shall not steal'? God meant what He said. I know He wants you to take this back."

I shook my head. "No way! I can't! I'm scared!"

"I'll go with you," Mr. T said. "We'll go around to the back."

Mr. T walked ahead with
giant steps. I had to run to keep up.

At the back of the stereo store,
Mr. T knocked. The owner opened the door and we
stepped inside. "I've come to pick up my
new TV," Mr. T said.

I hid the radio behind me. I looked at my feet. The owner stared at me.

"Go on," Mr. T said. "You're doin' the right thing."

I swallowed hard.

I set the silver box on the floor.

"I'm bringing this back!" I croaked.

"My radio!" the owner exclaimed.
Then he frowned. "But you
aren't the girl who took it."

I told him the whole story. I thought he would call the police. He called my folks instead. I sat down on a packing case to wait. I watched as Mr. T paid for his new TV. It was a special portable for his car. He lifted the set on one shoulder. On his way out, he stopped beside me.

"You gonna remember what I told you 'bout stealin'?" he asked.

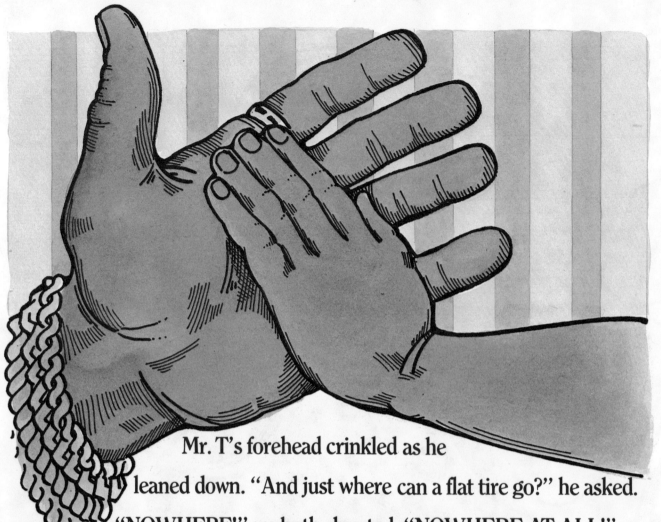

Mr. T's forehead crinkled as he
leaned down. "And just where can a flat tire go?" he asked.
"NOWHERE!" we both shouted. "NOWHERE AT ALL!"
Mr. T put his free hand out as his face broke into a big grin.
I reached out, too. And we clapped hands with a loud SLAP!

"NOWHERE!" he shouted. *"NOWHERE AT ALL!"*